Too Much Stuff!

Too Much Stuff!

Robert Munsch

illustrated by
Michael Martchenko

Scholastic Canada Ltd.
New York Toronto London Auckland Sydney
Mexico City New Delhi Hong Kong Buenos Aires

The illustrations in this book were painted in watercolour
on Crescent illustration board.
The type is set in 21 point Adobe Caslon Pro.

Scholastic Canada Ltd.
604 King Street West, Toronto, Ontario M5V 1E1, Canada

Scholastic Inc.
557 Broadway, New York, NY 10012, USA

Scholastic Australia Pty Limited
PO Box 579, Gosford, NSW 2250, Australia

Scholastic New Zealand Limited
Private Bag 94407, Botany, Manukau 2163, New Zealand

Scholastic Children's Books
Euston House, 24 Eversholt Street, London NW1 1DB, UK

www.scholastic.ca

Library and Archives Canada Cataloguing in Publication
Munsch, Robert N., 1945-
Too much stuff! / Robert Munsch ; illustrated by Michael Martchenko.

For children ages 3-8.
ISBN 978-1-4431-0245-2

I. Martchenko, Michael II. Title.

PS8576.U575T66 2010b   jC813'.54   C2010-904599-8

13 12 11 10 9   Printed in Malaysia   108   17 18 19 20 21

For Temina Girod,
Cold Lake, Alberta.
— *R.M.*

The day before she went to see Grandma, Temina said, "Dolls! Dolls! Dolls! I can take all my dolls on the airplane."

"One!" said her mom. "You can bring just one doll."

"Pleeeeeeease," said Temina. "I will be very sad without ALL my dolls."

"One!" said her mom. "You can bring just one doll. You can't bring ALL your dolls. You must have 500 dolls."

"HA!" said Temina. "I have just 37 dolls. You know that I have just 37 dolls, not 500 dolls."

"One!" said Temina's mom. "You can bring just one doll."

"OK! OK! OK!" said Temina.

Then Temina said, "Toys! Toys! Toys! I can take my toys. I want to take all my toys!"

"One!" said her mom. "You can bring just one toy."

"Pleeeeeeease," said Temina. "I will be very sad without ALL my toys."

"One!" said her mom. "You can bring just one toy. You can't bring all your toys. You must have 500 toys."

"HA!" said Temina. "I have just 37 toys. You know that I have just 37 toys, not 500 toys."

"One!" said Temina's mom. "You can bring just one toy."

"OK! OK! OK!" said Temina.

So when Temina came to the airport, she was carrying ONE doll and ONE toy.

She was also carrying a backpack that had 20 dolls and 20 toys in it, but her mom did not know about those 20 dolls and 20 toys. Temina got her little sister to help her stomp and cram and squish the dolls and toys till they fit into the backpack.

The backpack was very heavy, and Temina had trouble keeping up.

"Come on! Come on! Come on!" said her mom. "You are taking **FOREVER.** Let me carry your backpack."

8

"No!" said Temina. "MY backpack is MY backpack, and I will carry it!"

"Come on! Come on! Come on!" said her little sister. "You are taking **FOREVER.** Let me help you with your backpack."

"No!" said Temina. "MY backpack is MY backpack, and I will carry it!"

Finally they got in a long line.

A security officer said to Temina's mom, "Can I look in your backpack?"

"Yes," said Temina's mom.

Then he said to Temina's little sister, "Can I look in your backpack?"

"Yes," said her little sister.

Then he said to Temina, "Can I look in your backpack?"

"No!" said Temina. "You may NOT look in my backpack. My backpack is Top Secret."

"Right," said the officer. "How about we X-ray your backpack?"

"Well," said Temina, "You can do that, but do NOT tell my mom what is in it."

The officer put the backpack into the X-ray machine. Then he looked at the screen.

He yelled "AAAAAH!" and fell over.

All the other officers looked at the screen, yelled "AAAAAH!" and fell over.

Temina put her backpack back on and followed her mother and her little sister.

On the plane, the flight attendant said, "What's in the backpack?"

"Watch!" said Temina, and she unzipped it.

All the dolls and toys unscrunched and uncrammed and went flying all over the airplane:

KAFOOSHHHHH!

The airplane captain and all the other flight attendants came running.

"It's just my dolls and toys," yelled Temina.

"Right," they all said. "Dolls and toys. No problem." And they all went away again.

Then Temina put ten dolls and toys on the seat in front of her, and five on her seat, and three on the back of the seat, and ten on the ceiling with tape, and more wherever there was room.

"WOW!" said the flight attendant. "Lots of stuff!"

After they took off, the flight attendant came and said, "There are three kids from China and they will not stop crying because their mother did not let them bring their dolls and toys. Can I please borrow three of yours?"

"Yes," said Temina.

After a while the flight attendant came back again and said, "There are three kids from Kenya and they will not stop crying because their mother did not let them bring their dolls and toys. Can I please borrow three more of yours?"

"Yes," said Temina.

After a while the flight attendant came back again and said, "There are three kids from Scotland and they will not stop crying because their mother did not let them bring their dolls and toys. Can I please borrow three more of yours?"

"Yes," said Temina.
Then they watched a movie.
Then they had dinner.
Then Temina went to the bathroom 25 times.
Then everybody went to sleep.

When the plane landed, Temina woke up and ran off the plane to see her grandma.

Temina did not get back her dolls or toys. Happily, Temina's grandma made excellent dolls and toys, and she made Temina some new ones.

Temina forgot all about her lost dolls and toys.

Three months later the mailman brought Temina three packages.

One package was from China.

One package was from Scotland.

One package was from Kenya.

"WOW!" said Temina. "Who do I know in China? Who do I know in Scotland? Who do I know in Kenya?"

Temina opened the package from China and there was a Chinese doll.

Temina opened the package from Scotland and there was a Scottish doll.

Temina opened the package from Kenya and there was a Kenyan doll.

"Wow, Mom!" said Temina. "I can't wait to go on another plane ride. It is a great way to get new stuff!"

"HA!" said Temina's mom. "Next time, you go with your DAD."